Billie B. Brown

www.BillieBBrownBooks.com

For Hilary

Billie B. Brown Books

The Bad Butterfly
The Soccer Star
The Midnight Feast
The Second-best Friend
The Extra-special Helper
The Beautiful Haircut
The Big Sister
The Spotty Vacation
The Birthday Mix-up
The Secret Message
The Little Lie
The Best Project
The Deep End
The Copycat Kid
The Night Fright

First American Edition 2013
Kane Miller, A Division of EDC Publishing

Text Copyright © 2011 Sally Rippin
Illustrations Copyright © 2011 Aki Fukuoka
Logo and design copyright © 2011 Hardie Grant Egmont

First published in Australia in 2011 by Hardie Grant Egmont

For information contact:
Kane Miller, A Division of EDC Publishing
P.O. Box 470663
Tulsa, OK 74147-0663
www.kanemiller.com
www.edcpub.com
www.usbornebooksandmore.com

Library of Congress Control Number: 2012956111

Printed and bound in the United States of America
8 9 10
ISBN: 978-1-61067-184-2

The Big Sister

By Sally Rippin

Illustrated by Aki Fukuoka

Kane Miller
A DIVISION OF EDC PUBLISHING

Chapter One

Billie B. Brown has four baby jumpsuits, three tiny dresses and one big teddy bear. Do you know what the "B" in Billie B. Brown stands for?

Baby!

Billie's mom is having a baby. Billie is going to be a big sister!

These little clothes used to be Billie's. Aren't they tiny? They will be perfect for the new baby.

Billie is very **excited** about being a big sister.

2

Four baby jumpsuits

Three tiny dresses

One big teddy bear

3

She's going to give the baby her favorite teddy, Mr. Fred. Isn't that nice of her?

Billie has had Mr. Fred since she was a baby. But when the baby comes she won't need him anymore.

Today Billie is playing mommies and daddies with her best friend, Jack.

Jack lives next door.
Billie and Jack have
been friends since they
were little. They do
everything together.

Billie and Jack sit in the
fort they have made.
Billie squeezes Mr. Fred
into a pink dress.
He looks very funny.
Billie and Jack giggle.

Today it is Jack's turn to
watch the baby while
Billie goes off to work.

"I'm glad you're home," says Jack when Billie comes back. "Mr. Fred has been crying all day!"

Billie laughs and takes Mr. Fred. "I'm bored with playing mommies and daddies," she says. "Let's go and play soccer."

Jack and Billie run into the backyard to play.

Billie sits Mr. Fred on the grass to watch.

Oh dear. Look at those gray clouds.

Soon it starts to rain.

Billie and Jack run inside.
But they forget someone.

Poor Mr. Fred! He is
going to get very wet,
isn't he?

Chapter Two

That night, Billie's mom reads her a story in bed. It is about a mommy elephant and her baby. It is Billie's favorite book.

Suddenly Billie's mom stops reading. She gets a funny look on her face.

"Oh!" she says. "I think the baby is coming!"

She calls to Billie's dad.

Billie climbs out of bed
and helps her mom
downstairs. Billie's dad
rushes around finding all
the things they will need
for the hospital.

Suddenly Billie gets a
funny feeling in her
tummy. "Can I come
with you?" she says.

"No, sweetheart," says her dad. "Remember, we said that you will stay at Jack's house when the baby comes."

"How long will you be?" asks Billie, feeling **worried**.

"I don't know, Billie," says her mom.

She squeezes Billie's hand.
"But just think – next
time you see me, you will
have a little baby brother
or sister!"

But Billie has decided
she doesn't want a silly
old baby anymore.
She wants her mommy!
Billie scrunches up her
face and tries not to cry.

"It's all right, Billie," says her dad gently.

Jack's mom comes over to pick up Billie. They watch Billie's mom and dad drive off.

Billie's mom blows a kiss, but Billie looks down at the ground. She doesn't want them to go without her.

Jack's mom gives Billie a
cuddle. "I've made a bed
for you in Jack's room," she
says. They walk next door.

Jack is already asleep.
His mom tucks Billie
into the guest bed.

Jack's room looks strange in the dark. Billie wishes she was back in her own bed.

Suddenly she sits up.

"Mr. Fred!" she whispers. "I need Mr. Fred!"

"Oh dear. We'll get him tomorrow," says Jack's mom.

"How about you sleep with one of Jack's toys tonight?"

Jack's mom gives Billie a big blue teddy bear. He is very soft and cuddly. But he's not like Mr. Fred.

Billie lies in the dark. Her tummy is curling up with **worry**.

She can't remember
where she put Mr. Fred!

You remember where he
is though, don't you?

Chapter Three

The next day, Billie
has breakfast with Jack's
family. But she doesn't
feel very hungry.

Just then there is a knock
on the door. It's Billie's dad!

"Billie!" he says excitedly.
"Guess what? You have a
baby brother!"

"A brother?" Billie says,
frowning. "But I wanted
a sister! Who will wear all
my baby dresses now?"

"Oh, Billie," says her dad,
giving her a cuddle.
"You should see him.

He's beautiful! And I'm sure he'll look lovely in your pretty pink dresses."

Billie giggles. "Where's Mom?" she asks. "Is she coming home now?"

"Not yet," her dad says. "Mom has to rest. She will be at the hospital for a few days. But we can go and see her."

"A few days!" Billie says crossly. "But I want Mom to come home now." She **stamps** her foot.

Billie's dad sighs.

He thanks Jack's parents
for taking care of Billie.
Billie and her dad go
back home for Billie to
get dressed.

Billie feels all jumbled up
inside. She is **excited** to
see her new baby brother.
But she also feels a
teensy bit **cross** that
he is a boy, not a girl.

She is **excited** to see her mom, but she is also **cross** that her mom is not coming home yet. All these feelings bubble up inside Billie's tummy like a milkshake.

Then she remembers.

"Mr. Fred!" she says.
"I have to find Mr. Fred
to give to the new baby!"

"OK," says her dad.
"But quickly. Mom is
waiting for us."

Billie looks everywhere for
Mr. Fred. She looks under
her bed. No Mr. Fred.
Then she checks her
toy box. Not there either!

She checks all the
places Mr. Fred could be.
But he is nowhere to
be found.

"We have to go now,"
Billie's dad says. "We can
give Mr. Fred to the baby
next time."

"No!" says Billie. "I want Mr. Fred!" She **stamps** her feet.

"Billie!" says her dad. He is looking very tired. "Come on. You have to be a big girl now."

"But I don't want to be a big girl!" Billie cries. "I want to be a baby too!"

Billie's dad bends down
and gives her a big hug.

"It's OK," he says gently.
"You will always be my
baby girl, Billie. Now how
about we go see Mom?

We can look for Mr. Fred
again when we get
home."

Billie stops crying and
gives her dad a big cuddle.

Chapter Four

Billie and her dad arrive
at the hospital. Her mom
is sitting up in bed.
She holds out her arms
and Billie jumps onto the
bed for a cuddle.

Billie's mom points to a plastic crib next to the bed. "There's your little brother," she says. "His name is Noah. Isn't he adorable?"

Billie looks into the plastic crib. Noah is wrapped up like a fat white caterpillar. His face is all squishy and red. He doesn't look very adorable to Billie.

"Would you like to hold him?" her mom asks.

"Nah," says Billie snuggling up to her mom. "Maybe later."

Billie's mom lets her change
the channels on the TV.
Then Billie tells her mom
about poor lost Mr. Fred.

Soon it is time to go.
Billie kisses her mom
goodbye. She even gives
Noah a kiss. He smells nice.
Like banana pancakes!

"Bye-bye, baby!" Billie
says softly.

Just then Noah opens
his eyes. He looks
straight up at Billie.
A little smile creeps over
his tiny face. Then he
closes his eyes again.

"He smiled at me!"
Billie gasps.

"Wow, Billie! You're the first person he's smiled at," her mom says.

"That's because he knows you're his big sister," her dad says.

Billie feels very **proud**. She is the first person her baby brother has smiled at.

He likes her! Maybe it will be fun to be a big sister after all.

"OK, time to go," says her dad. "Let's go home and look for Mr. Fred, shall we?"

When they get home, Jack is waiting on Billie's front doorstep.

He has something in his arms. Something big and furry and wet and muddy.

"Mr. Fred!" Billie says.

"Oh dear," says her dad. "Did you leave him out in the rain?"

Billie nods. She gives poor old Mr. Fred a big cuddle.

She has missed him so much!

"I don't think I want to give Mr. Fred to Noah anymore," Billie says.

"After all, Mr. Fred is a bit old and dirty for our new baby."

Billie knows that being a big sister will be fun most days. But some days she might want to be a baby, too. She will need Mr. Fred on those days.

"But what will you give the baby?" Jack asks.

Billie smiles. "Our new baby needs a *new* teddy bear," she says. "Just for him!"

Then she giggles. "And do you know what else? I think Mr. Fred needs a bath!"

Collect them all!

Billie B. Brown

The Bad Butterfly
By Sally Rippin

Billie B. Brown

The Soccer Star
By Sally Rippin

Billie B. Brown

The Midnight Feast
By Sally Rippin

Billie B. Brown

The Second-best Friend
By Sally Rippin

Billie B. Brown

The Extra-special Helper
By Sally Rippin

Billie B. Brown

The Beautiful Haircut
By Sally Rippin

Billie B. Brown

The Big Sister
By Sally Rippin

Billie B. Brown

The Spotty Vacation
By Sally Rippin

Billie B. Brown

The Birthday Mix-up
By Sally Rippin

Billie B. Brown

The Secret Message
By Sally Rippin

Billie B. Brown

The Little Lie
By Sally Rippin

Billie B. Brown

The Best Project
By Sally Rippin

Billie B. Brown

The Deep End
By Sally Rippin

Billie B. Brown

The Copycat Kid
By Sally Rippin

Billie B. Brown

The Night Fright
By Sally Rippin